A Ghost Story

Nina Crews

Greenwillow Books *An Imprint of* HarperCollins*Publishers*

For my nephew, Jack.

Special thanks to Zachary, Alexa, Kathy, Geddis, and Patrick Williams, who brought this story to life as Jonathan, Celeste, their mother, their father, and Uncle Pete. Thanks also to Wilma McDaniel and Joan McDaniel; and thanks to Jonathan Williams, who played patiently downstairs.

Full-color 35-mm photographs were
digitally color-corrected and manipulated
using Adobe Photoshop™ and Adobe
Illustrator™.
The text type is Franklin Gothic Book.

Library of Congress
Cataloging-in-Publication Data
Crews, Nina.
A ghost story / by Nina Crews.
    p.   cm.
"Greenwillow Books."
Summary: When Uncle Pete comes
to visit, he listens to Celeste's singing
and helps Jonathan get rid of the ghost
that's been causing so much trouble.
ISBN 0-688-17673-9 (trade).
ISBN 0-688-17674-7 (lib. bdg.)
[1. Uncles—Fiction.
2. Family life—Fiction.
3. Afro-Americans—Fiction.] I. Title.
PZ7.C8683 Gh 2001
[E]—dc21 00-037122

1 2 3 4 5 6 7 8 9 10
First Edition

Ghost

CRREEAKK!!!!

Things creak in
my house.
My mother tells
me that it's
because the
house is old.
She says,
"Old houses
creak, just like
old bones."

But I know
she's wrong.
Because I see
things that
she can't see.
I listen to
those creaks,
and I hear
whispering.

We have a ghost in the house.
It rattles the doors.
It knocks our books on the floor.
It chases our cat around in circles.

My father thinks I do these things. He says, "Stop fooling around. Pick up those books and leave the cat alone."

My sister, Celeste, is always singing. She never notices anything. I tell her about the ghost and she says, "Don't bother me. I'm busy practicing."

The ghost visits me at night when I can't fall
asleep. It sits at the foot of my bed. I talk to
it about important things. About my friends,
school, and my annoying sister. I talk about
my Uncle Pete, who lives out west. He's
coming to visit on May 1st.

Some nights the ghost gets really cranky.
It shakes the bed and makes my teddy bear
float in the air. It flickers the lights on and off.
I have to yell at it. I shout, **"STOP!"**

Then my parents call from the next room,
"Jonathan, be quiet. You'll wake up your
little sister. Go to sleep."

But I can't sleep. There's a ghost in the house.
And it's always getting me into trouble.
I just wish someone else could see it, too.

I am a jazz singer.
Everybody always
tells me that I have
a wonderful
singing voice.
I perform
almost nightly.
I am very famous.

Fame is a difficult
thing sometimes.
My brother is jealous.
And he gets angry
when I practice my
scales in public.

He's always
distracting me,
then blaming it on
some crazy ghost.
He calls me
a show-off.

I'm not. I'm just
committed to
my craft.

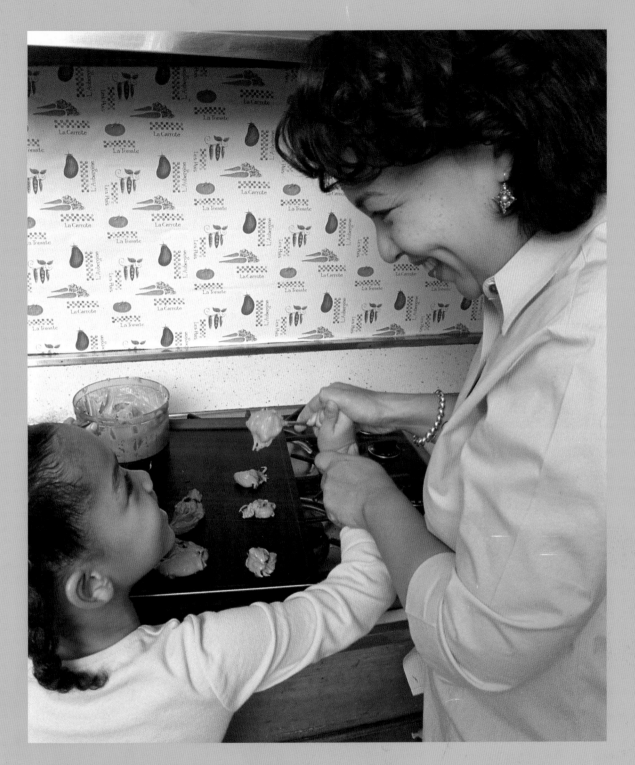

Our Uncle Pete is coming to visit. I am going to sing for him. My mother and I are baking cookies. My daddy is helping me make the tickets and the programs. It will be my best show ever.

I'm practicing my scales
constantly and learning
all new songs.
I can't wait.

On Saturday
May 1st

I'm so excited. Uncle Pete will be here soon!
His plane lands at one o'clock, and there's
still so much to do.

I'm helping in the kitchen. I'm cleaning up my room.

Celeste is supposed to be putting away her toys, but she keeps trying on dresses.

My mother sends us to the corner store for eggs, juice, and butter. Celeste won't stop singing.

He's here!

"Hey, Jonathan! You've grown," says Uncle Pete. "And look at you, little baby girl—looking like a lady."

I start telling Uncle Pete six stories at once. I talk so fast that I'm out of breath.

Uncle Pete smiles. "Well, Jonathan, I see you and I have some catching up to do. We're going to have to spend a lot of time together."

Later that afternoon Celeste shouts,
"Is everybody ready for my concert?
Uncle Pete, did you purchase your ticket?
Lights!" She starts off with scales, as usual,
and then a couple of off-key songs.

Mommy grins from ear to ear and Daddy
is smiling, too.

"Yeah, Celeste!" cheers Uncle Pete.
"That was great! What a star!"

I guess she sounded all right.

At dinner my father starts teasing me. "Jonathan, why don't you tell Pete about your ghost?"

"Jonathan's been seeing and hearing all sorts of strange things," says Mommy.

"And getting into lots of trouble," says Celeste.

I change the subject. "Uncle Pete, I wish you lived here with us. Why did you have to move?"

"I know you all thought I was crazy to go so far away," says Uncle Pete. "But this move was just what I needed."

UNCLE PETE
OUT WEST

I live in a little house on a dirt road about a mile outside of town. I just got a horse. You can help me name it. I have two dogs, Acey and Malone. Every morning, I take a walk and look around. It's just me, my animals, some rocks, and cactus.

On weekends I like to go for horseback rides or hikes in the dry, rocky hills and canyons. I'm sure there are some ghosts out there. There's an oasis I like to go to, with tall, old palm trees.

The palm trees whisper in the wind. Birds fly overhead. Squirrels chatter back and forth. I just sit and listen.

It's a different world.

When you come out to visit, we'll go
horseback riding. We'll ride through
canyons and to the river. We'll take
my dogs. We'll look for rabbits.
We'll do it soon.

Ghost
Fly Free

"It's getting late," says Daddy.
"Time for you kids to go to bed."

"I'll tuck you in," says Uncle Pete.

He goes into Celeste's room first.
Now they're both singing!

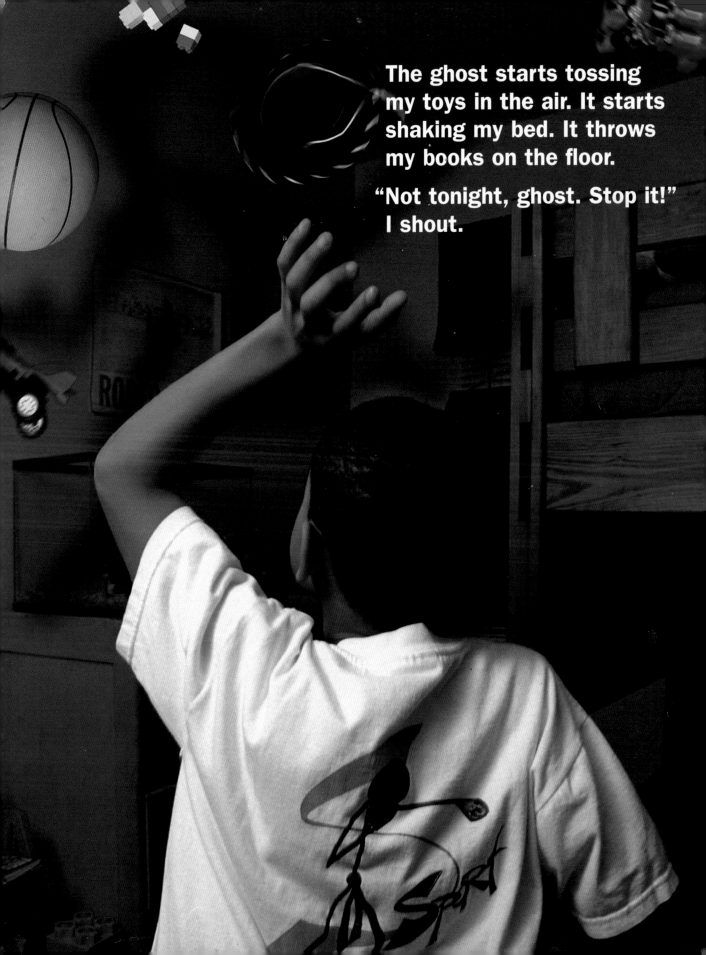

The ghost starts tossing my toys in the air. It starts shaking my bed. It throws my books on the floor.

"Not tonight, ghost. Stop it!" I shout.

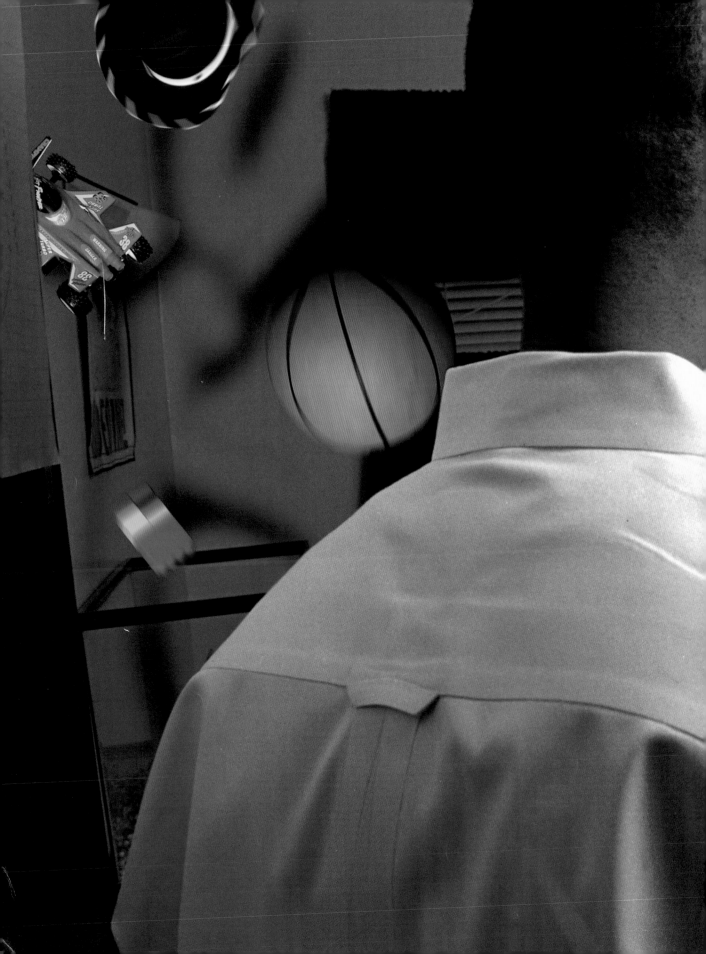

"Hey, Jonathan?" Uncle Pete pokes his head into my room. "What is going on in here?"

The ghost hovers in a corner.

"It's throwing my things on the floor," I say. "It never behaves. Dumb ghost."

"Ghost?!" he says. "I thought they were just teasing you at dinner. Ghosts can be trouble, you know."

"Yeah," I say. "This one sure is."
I look around. My basketball's in the fish tank, and my cowboy poster is torn. Then I look at Uncle Pete.

"Do you want me to help you get rid of it?" he asks.

I nod.

"Well, I haven't chased ghosts for a while, but I'll try." Uncle Pete grabs the sheet from the bed. He gives it to me. "See if you can throw this over it."

The ghost swoops up to the ceiling and down to the floor.

It goes left, right, and left again.

It goes round and round in circles.

I throw the sheet once. I miss. I throw it again—

"I've got it!" I shout.

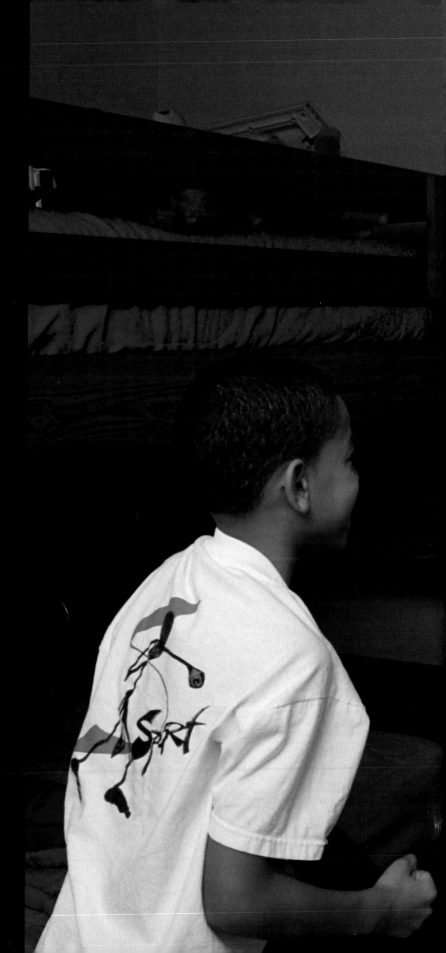

Great!" says Uncle Pete. "Now pass it to me." He wraps the sheet up tight. This ghost must be lost. It sure doesn't belong here. Let's see if we can send it on its way. You open the window. Okay now, shout with me—

ONE, TWO, THREE! GHOST FLY FREE!"

Uncle Pete shakes the sheet and the ghost out of the window.

Then he shuts it quick.

I look outside. I see the trees rustling.
I hear a car alarm honking. A plastic
bag floats up into the air. Then I hear
a whisper. *"Thank you."*

After

After that the house was quiet. The books stayed on the bookshelves, and my toys stayed on my bed. Uncle Pete said he'd chase ghosts with me anytime. We spent a lot of time together. He took me to the movies. He sang songs with Celeste.

We named his horse Brooklyn. We'll see him soon.

Now when I can't fall asleep, and need someone to talk to, I go into my parents' room and talk with them for a while. Then I come back to my room and climb into bed.

And there are no more ghosts.